Table of Contents

Rourke Educational Media

rourkeeducationalmedia.com

Can you find these words?

better

growth

start

together

Mount Rushmore

A symbol stands for an idea.

Mount Rushmore is in South Dakota.

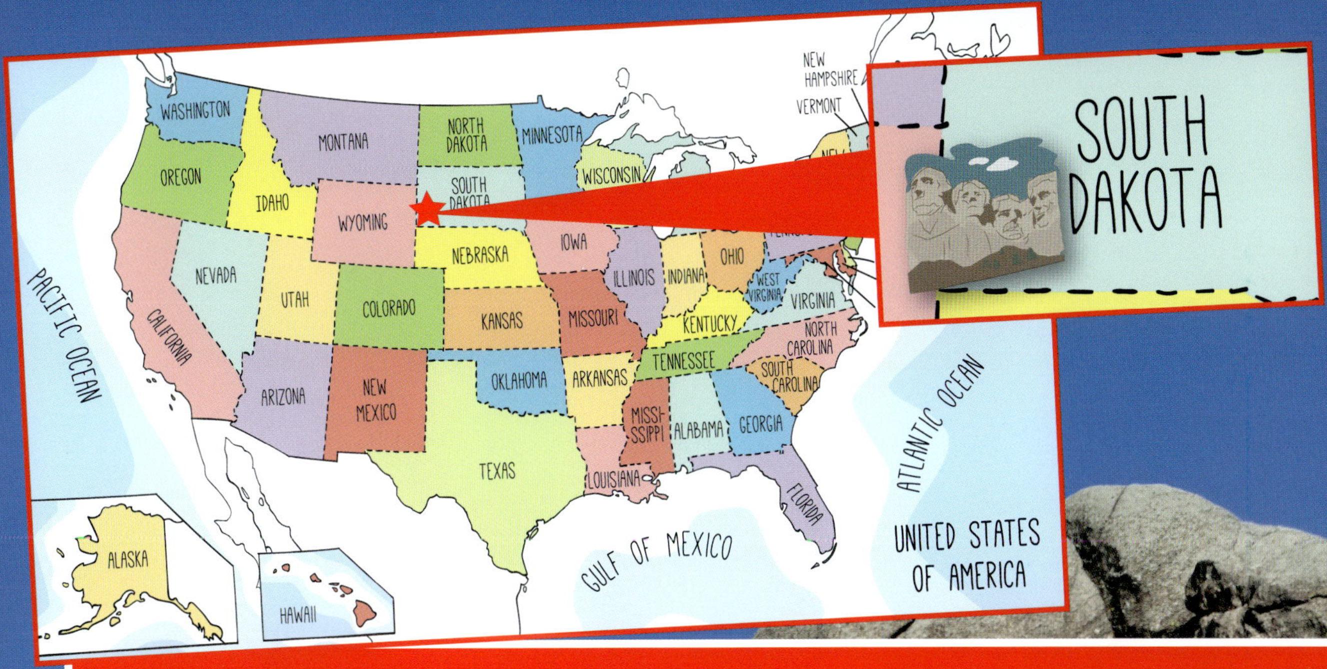

It is a symbol of the United States.

Four U.S. presidents are carved there. Each is a symbol of the country's history.

George Washington is a symbol of the country's **start**.

Thomas Jefferson is a symbol of the country's **growth**.

Abraham Lincoln is a symbol of the country staying **together**.

Theodore Roosevelt is a symbol of the country getting **better**.

Did you find these words?

Theodore Roosevelt is a symbol of the country getting **better**.

Thomas Jefferson is a symbol of the country's **growth**.

George Washington is a symbol of the country's **start**.

Abraham Lincoln is a symbol of the country staying **together**.

Photo Glossary

better (BET-ur): Become improved or more suitable.

growth (grohth): The process of becoming bigger, more mature, or more valuable.

start (stahrt): A place or time when something begins.

together (tuh-GETH-ur): With one another or as one group.

Index

About the Author

K.A. Robertson is a writer and editor who enjoys learning about the history of the United States. Her favorite presidents are Abraham Lincoln and Barack Obama.

www.rourkeeducationalmedia.com

PHOTO CREDITS: Cover, p4,6: ©RiverNorthPhotography; p2, 13,14,15: ©Library of Congress; The Crowley Company; p2,9,14,15: John Trumball; p2,7,14,15: ©jaflippo; p2,10,14,15: ©wikimedia; p3: ©wundervisuals; p12: ©zrfphoto; p13: ©lukbar

Edited by: Keli Sipperley
Cover and interior design by: Kathy Walsh

Library of Congress PCN Data
Mount Rushmore / K.A. Robertson
(Visiting U.S. Symbols)
ISBN 978-1-64369-057-5 (hard cover)(alk. paper)
ISBN 978-1-64369-081-0 (soft cover)
ISBN 978-1-64369-204-3 (e-Book)
Library of Congress Control Number: 2018955884

Printed in the United States of America, North Mankato, Minnesota